Santa Pups

by Jerry Pallotta
illustrated by Will Terry

SCHOLASTIC INC.

To Maeve Pallotta and Hazel Butterworth.
— J.P.

For all the dogs in my life: Rusty, Sadie, Cammy, and Pooch.
— W.T.

ISBN 978-0-545-48479-4

Text copyright © 2013 by Jerry Pallotta. Illustrations copyright © 2013 by Will Terry.
All rights reserved. Published by Scholastic Inc.
SCHOLASTIC and associated logos are trademarks and/or registered trademarks of Scholastic Inc.

12 11 10 9 8 7 6 5 4 3 2 1   14 15 16 17 18 19/0

Printed in the U.S.A.   40

First Scholastic paperback printing, November 2014

Santa loved his reindeer. But one year
he wanted to let someone else pull his sleigh.

He decided to give some stray dogs a try.

What kind of dog
would be best?

First Santa tried poodles.

They were always having their nails done.

He gave
Labradors a
chance.

All they did was make noise.

He hooked up the Pekingese.

The sleigh didn't even budge.

He tried a few mastiffs.

Too big.
Way too big!

And they ate too much.

He hitched some pit bulls to the sled.

It was exhausting! All they did was argue.

Santa used a bunch of Shar-Peis.

They looked too wrinkled
for the North Pole
Christmas card.

The Dalmatians hurt Santa's eyes.

He kept seeing spots everywhere.

The dachshunds made him hungry.

All he could think of were hot dogs with mustard and relish.

Santa tested basset hounds.

They looked
too sad.

The greyhounds were too fast.

He was afraid of getting
a speeding ticket.

Santa tried sheepdogs.

He couldn't tell where
they were looking.

Santa considered
a pack of mutts.

It was a bumpy ride.

Santa loved each
and every dog.

He decided to adopt them all.

But maybe next year he'll try cats.